MW00912095

MOMMY POEMS

Compiled by John Micklos, Jr.

Illustrated by
Lori McElrath-Eslick

Wordsong
Boyds Mills Press

To my mother and my wife, the two best mommies I know.

—J. M., Jr.

To my baby boy Chase with love,
you made me a mommy again.

—L. M. E.

Collection copyright © 2001 by John Micklos, Jr.
Illustrations copyright © 2001 by Lori McElrath-Eslick
All rights reserved

Published by Wordsong
Boyds Mills Press, Inc.
A Highlights Company
815 Church Street
Honesdale, Pennsylvania 18431
Printed in China

U.S. Cataloging-in-Publication Data
(Library of Congress Standards)

Micklos, John.
 Mommy poems / selected by John Micklos, Jr. ; illustrated by Lori
McElrath-Eslick. —1st ed.
[32]p. : col. ill. ; cm.
Summary: Poems in celebration of motherhood.
ISBN 1-56397-849-0   Hardcover
ISBN 1-56397-908-X   Paperback
1. Mothers — Poetry. 2. Mother and child — Poetry. 3. American
poetry — Collections.
I. Micklos, John. II. McElrath-Eslick, Lori, ill. III. Title.
811/.54 21 2001 CIP   AC
99-63912

First edition, 2001
Book designed by Jennifer Neal.
The text of this book is set in 15-point Berkeley.

10 9 8 7 6 5 4 3 2   Hardcover
10 9 8 7 6 5 4 3 2 1   Paperback

Table of Contents

My Name

I wrote my name on the sidewalk
But the rain washed it away.

I wrote my name on my hand
But the soap washed it away.

I wrote my name on the birthday card
I gave to Mother today

And there it will stay
For Mother never throws

ANYTHING

of mine away!

Lee Bennett Hopkins

Waiting for Mommy to Wake Up

I stand in the dark,
right here
beside your warm feet.

I open my eyes
as big as I can
      so you can see me.

I wiggle your foot
     —just a little.

I feel your sleepy frown
     looking at me.

Then I think I see
one side of your mouth
bend a little.

You hold up the blanket
and scoot to
     the cold edge of the bed.
I scramble inside the little tunnel you make
and feel the
     warm spot
     you gave up
       just for me.

And all the cold
     and the scariness
     flies back
to my lonely bed.

Jane Medina

Cuddle Time

On winter mornings I wake up early
And bounce out of bed,
Racing to my mother's room,
My feet barely touching the cold wood floor.
I pull back the covers
Of her big, deep feather bed
And dive in, giggling.
She laughs, too, a sleepy laugh.
Then we cuddle together, toasty warm,
Safe in our own little cocoon,
Preparing for our butterfly journey
Into the day.
Two bodies so close
They seem like one—
Mommy and me.

John Micklos, Jr.

Dinner and Dessert

We're having WHAT for dinner, Mom?
You know I don't like that!
Don't even put it on my plate.
Just feed it to the cat.

Don't scold or plead or threaten me.
Those tricks will surely fail.
Just serve me something else instead.
I'd rather eat a whale.

You say, "No dinner, no dessert."
That argument's no good.
There's no dessert that's good enough
To make me eat this food!

We're having WHAT for our dessert?
My favorite chocolate cake!
With that special, secret icing
That you hardly ever make!

Well, I GUESS I'll eat my dinner
Even if it makes me hurt,
But I'll need to save some space so
That I'll have room for dessert.

John Micklos, Jr.

Mending

She pokes, then pulls
the thin blue thread
through daddy's shirt.
(Over, under, down and through,
the silver needle pulling blue.)
The long tail swims
in and out of plaid;
dad needs his shirt
first thing for work.
(Inside, out, she yanks it tight;
thread, needle, lap, light—)
until that button's
back on
right.

Rebecca Kai Dotlich

Going Out to Tea

Mommy's dressing me all up
With flowers everywhere.
She's washed my hands.
She's washed my face.
She's even curled my hair.

She's made me wear my daisy hat.
She bought me lacy gloves.
She's dabbed perfume
Behind my ears
—The kind she really loves.

And now we're getting
In the car.
She's taking me to tea.
I'm bringing my doll, Missy.
I guess her doll
        is ME!

Jane Medina

Mother, May I?

Mother, may I
take a giant step?

Or two?

> One
> little
> one,
> very small,
> will do.

I'm falling behind!
Look at my friends!

> So you have to do *everything*
> they do, then?

Upset all my plans!
You're mean!
You're so cruel!

> It's the way of the world:
> Mothers rule.

Janet S. Wong

The Keeper of Dreams

When I grow up, I want to be
A sailor sailing on the sea—
Or maybe a teacher,
Or maybe a singer,
Or maybe a preacher,
Or a steeple bell ringer.

You could be all those things,
My mom says to me.
You can be anything
That you want to be.
Just follow your dreams,
Wherever they lead,
For life is a tree and
Your dreams are the seeds.

When you're young, you can dream
Of being anything—
An actor, a rock star,
An athlete, a king.
Whatever I wish for,
No matter how hard it seems,
I share with my mother,
The keeper of dreams.

John Micklos, Jr.

14

Flavors

Mama is chocolate: you must be swirls
                                of dark fudge,
                    and ripples
                                            through
                        your cocoa
                                    curls;
chips
        and
flips of sprinkles
        on your
                summer
                face.

Arnold Adoff

Bad, Mad, Sad, Glad

Sometimes when I'm bad, bad, bad
My mother sends me off to bed.

Then I get so mad, mad, mad
I stamp my feet and shake my head.

When I calm down, I'm sad, sad, sad.
Mom asks what I'm crying about.

Soon we are both glad, glad, glad
When we have talked and worked things out.

John Micklos, Jr.

Ode to Family Photographs

This is the pond, and these are my feet.
This is the rooster, and this is more of my feet.

Mamá was never good at pictures.

This is a statue of a famous general who lost an arm,
And this is me with my head cut off.

This is a trash can chained to a gate,
This is my father with his eyes half-closed.

This is a photograph of my sister
And a giraffe looking over her shoulder.

This is our car's front bumper.
This is a bird with a pretzel in its beak.
This is my brother Pedro standing on one leg on a rock,
With a smear of chocolate on his face.

Mamá sneezed when she looked
Behind the camera: the snapshots are blurry,
The angles dizzy as a spin on a merry-go-round.

But we had fun when Mamá picked up the camera.
How can I tell?
Each of us laughing hard.
Can you see? I have candy in my mouth.

Gary Soto

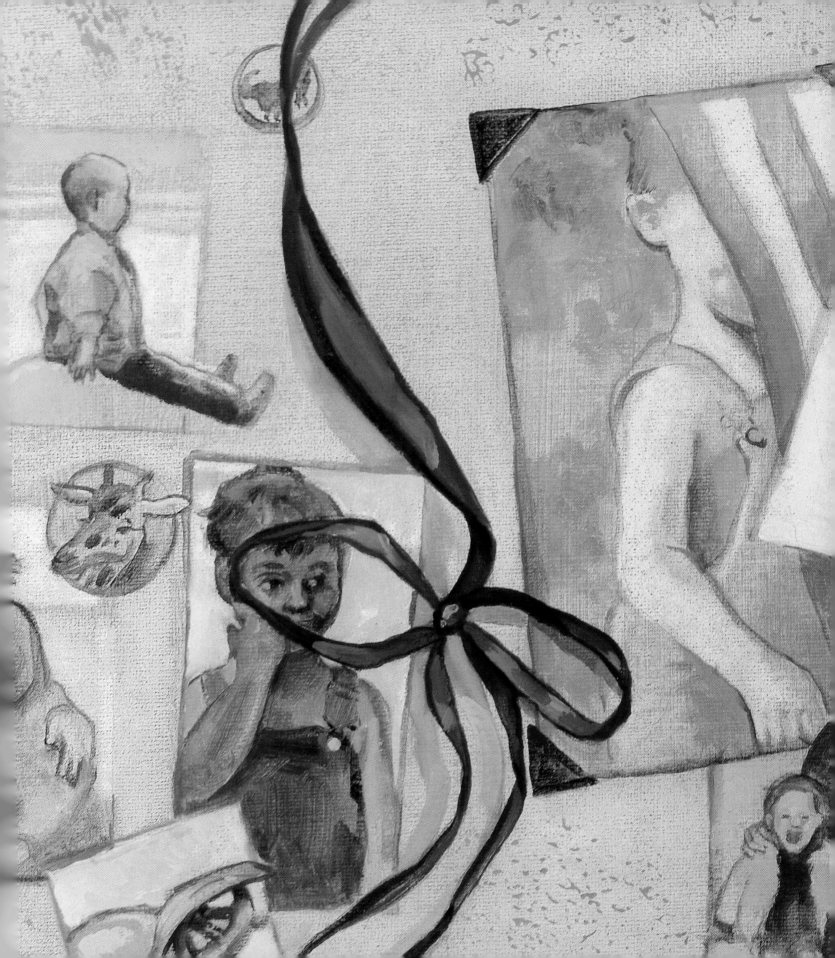

Sick Days

On days when I am sick in bed
My mother is so nice;
She brings me bowls of chicken soup
And ginger ale with ice.

She cuts the crusts off buttered toast
And serves it on a tray
And sits down while I eat it
And doesn't go away.

She reads my favorite books to me;
She lets me take my pick;
And everything is perfect—
Except that I am sick!

By Mary Ann Hoberman

Naptime

I never want to take my nap.
I'd rather play instead.
I want to run and jump outside,
Not lay down in my bed.

But Mommy reads my favorite book,
A naptime story treat.
Then she sings a lullaby.
Her voice is sugar sweet.

Her arms are warm and gentle,
The pillow soft and deep.
And then, before I know it,
I've drifted off to sleep.

By John Micklos, Jr.

New Mother

She came to take
my mother's
place.

I like her smile.

I like her face.

I like the way
    she talks to me
    although it's seldom
    we agree
        on bedtime
        or some places where
        I go.
            But then
    she seems to care.

    And often, when
    we both get mad
    and have to settle things
    with Dad

at least
we learn about each other.

I'm sort of getting used to—
Mother.

R. H. Marks

Sunday Drive with Mom

It's another Sunday drive—
just Mom and me, out for a spin.
Are we lost?

A winding road, and then
a curious turn—
Yes. We're lost.

Again.

Kristine O'Connell George

On Mother's Day

On Mother's Day we got up first,
so full of plans we almost burst.

We started breakfast right away
as our surprise for Mother's Day.

We picked some flowers, then hurried back
to make the coffee—rather black.

We wrapped our gifts and wrote a card
and boiled the eggs—a little hard.

And then we sang a serenade,
which burned the toast, I am afraid.

But Mother said, amidst our cheers,
"Oh, what a big surprise, my dears.
I've not had such a treat in years."
And she was smiling to her ears!

Aileen Fisher

Mommies

MOMMIES
make you brush your teeth
 and put your old clothes on
 and clean the room
 and call you from the playground
 and fuss at daddies and uncles
 and tuck you in at night
 and kiss you.

Nikki Giovanni

Tucking-In Song

Down the narrow hall she came,
 a symphony
 of jingle bells
 as tiny
 shiny
 silver charms
waltzed like wind-chimes
 on her arm,
 and haunting notes
 of tinkling tin
 played music on
 her perfumed skin . . .

When Mama came to tuck me in.

Rebecca Kai Dotlich

About the Poets

Arnold Adoff is a noted author, poet, and anthologist. His numerous books include *All the Colors of the Race*, in which "Flavors," his poem that appears in this book, was originally published.

Rebecca Kai Dotlich's poems have appeared in many children's magazines and in several anthologies. Her books for children include the poetry books *Sweet Dreams of the Wild* and *Lemonade Sun and Other Summer Poems*.

Aileen Fisher is a noted poet, whose awards include the NCTE Award for Excellence in Poetry for Children. "On Mother's Day," her poem that appears here, originally appeared in her book *Skip Around the Year*.

Kristine O'Connell George received the Lee Bennett Hopkins Promising Poet Award from the International Reading Association for her book *The Great Frog Race and Other Poems*, from which "Sunday Drive," her poem that appears here, is drawn.

Nikki Giovanni is a noted author and children's poet. Her numerous books include *Spin a Soft Black Song*, in which "Mommies," the poem in this book, originally appeared.

Mary Ann Hoberman is the author of many books for children. Her works include the award-winning book, *A House Is a House for Me*, and *Fathers, Mothers, Sisters, Brothers: A Collection of Family Poems*.

Lee Bennett Hopkins is one of the world's best-known poets and anthologists. His numerous books include the autobiographical *Been to Yesterdays*. "My Name," his poem in this book, is drawn from his book *Kim's Place and Other Poems*.

R. H. Marks is a pseudonym for Myra Cohn Livingston, the noted poet and anthologist. "New Mother," her poem in this book, was originally published in the book *Poems for Mothers*, which she compiled.

Jane Medina's poetry reflects the love she has developed for children, poetry, and education in more than twenty years as an elementary schoolteacher. She is the author of a poetry book titled *My Name is Jorge*.

John Micklos, Jr. has been an education writer and editor for more than twenty years. *Mommy Poems*, the second children's poetry book he has compiled, is a follow-up to his *Daddy Poems* collection.

Gary Soto is an award-winning author, poet, and essayist. "Ode to Family Photographs," his poem in this book, comes from his book *Neighborhood Odes*, about the neighborhood in which he grew up.

Janet S. Wong practiced law for a number of years before deciding to devote her time to writing. "Mother, May I?" her poem in this book, comes from her book *The Rainbow Hand: Poems About Mothers and Children*.

Acknowledgments

The compiler and publisher are grateful for permission to include the following copyrighted material. Every attempt has been made to locate and secure appropriate permissions for these works. If any errors or omissions have been made, corrections will be made in subsequent editions.

"My Name" by Lee Bennett Hopkins. Copyright © 1974 by Lee Bennett Hopkins. First appeared in *Kim's Place and Other Poems*, published by Holt, Rinehart and Winston. Reprinted by permission of Curtis Brown, Ltd.

"Cuddle Time," "Dinner and Dessert," "The Keeper of Dreams," "Bad, Mad, Sad, Glad," and "Nap Time" by John Micklos, Jr. Copyright © 2000 by John Micklos, Jr. Original poems.

"Tucking-In Song" by Rebecca Kai Dotlich. Copyright © 1997 by Rebecca Kai Dotlich. First appeared in *Song and Dance*, poems selected by Lee Bennett Hopkins, published by Simon & Schuster Books for Young Readers, 1997. Reprinted by permission of Curtis Brown, Ltd.

"Waiting for Mommy to Wake Up" and "Going Out to Tea" by Jane Medina. Copyright © 2000 by Jane Medina. Original poems.

"Mending" by Rebecca Kai Dotlich. Copyright © 2000 by Rebecca Kai Dotlich. Original poem. Reprinted by permission of Curtis Brown, Ltd.

"Mother, May I?" by Janet S. Wong. Reprinted with the permission of Margaret K. McElderry Books, an imprint of Simon & Schuster Children's Publishing Division, from *The Rainbow Hand* by Janet S. Wong. Text copyright © 1999 by Janet S. Wong.

"Flavors" by Arnold Adoff. Reprinted with the permission of Lothrop, Lee & Shepard, a division of HarperCollins Publishers, from *All the Colors of the Race: Poems by Arnold Adoff*. Text copyright © 1982 by Arnold Adoff.

"Ode to Family Photographs" by Gary Soto. From *Neighborhood Odes*, copyright © 1992 by Gary Soto, reprinted by permission of Harcourt, Inc.

"Sick Days" by Mary Ann Hoberman. From *Fathers, Mothers, Sisters, Brothers: A Collection of Family Poems* by Mary Ann Hoberman. Copyright © 1991 by Mary Ann Hoberman (text); copyright © 1991 by Marylin Hafner (illustrations). Reprinted by permission of Little, Brown and Company Inc.

"Sunday Drive with Mom" by Kristine O'Connell George. From *The Great Frog Race and Other Poems* by Kristine O'Connell George. Text copyright © 1997 by Kristine O'Connell George. Reprinted by permission of Clarion Books/Houghton Mifflin Company.

"On Mother's Day" by Aileen Fisher, copyright © 1967, 1995 by Aileen Fisher. From *Skip Around the Year* by Aileen Fisher, published by Harper and Row. Used by permission of Marian Reiner for the author.

"New Mother" by R. H. Marks, copyright © 1988 by R. H. Marks. First appeared in *Poems for Mothers*, edited by Myra Cohn Livingston, published by Holiday House. Used by permission of Marian Reiner.

"Mommies" from *Spin a Soft Black Song, Revised Edition* by Nikki Giovanni, illustrated by George Martins. Copyright © 1971, 1985 by Nikki Giovanni, reprinted by permission of Farrar, Straus and Giroux, LLC.